Arthur and the Nerves of Steal

A Marc Brown ARTHUR Chapter Book

Arthur and the Nerves of Steal

Text by Stephen Krensky

Based on a teleplay by Bruce Akiyama

 LITTLE, BROWN AND COMPANY

New York ᏸ Boston

Little, Brown and Company

Time Warner Book Group
1271 Avenue of the Americas, New York, NY 10020
Visit our Web site at www.lb-kids.com

First Edition

Text has been reviewed and assigned a reading level by Laurel S. Ernst,
M.A., Teachers College, Columbia University, New York, New York;
reading specialist, Chappaqua, New York.

Library of Congress Cataloging-in-Publication Data
Krensky, Stephen.
Arthur and the nerves of steal / text by Stephen Krensky ;
based on a teleplay by Bruce Akiyama. — 1st ed.
p.   cm. — (A Marc Brown Arthur chapter book ; 32)
Summary: When Buster impulsively drops a Cybertoy into Arthur's
backpack in the drugstore one day, he feels so guilty that he finally
confesses to his friend and they try to return the popular toy
before anyone else finds out.
ISBN 0-316-12618-7 (pb) — ISBN 0-316-12895-3 (hc)
[1. Stealing — Fiction.   2. Rabbits — Fiction.   3. Aardvark — Fiction.
4. Animals — Fiction.]   I. Akiyama, Bruce.   II. Title.
PZ7.K883Ark   2004
[Fic] — dc22   2003026600

10 9 8 7 6 5 4 3 2 1

WOR (hc)

COM-MO (pb)

Printed in the United States of America

To Linda Turrell

Chapter 1

• • • • • • • • • • •

Sir Buster let out a deep sigh.

Here he sat, looking out a window in the tower of Baxter Castle. It was a bright, sunny day, but Sir Buster could not enjoy the view. Other knights might be out fighting dragons or rescuing villagers in need. But not Sir Buster. He could not even stay busy polishing his armor or sharpening his sword. At the moment he was a defenseless prisoner. He had not been captured, though. He had not been defeated in battle. Sir Buster could not blame his troubles on someone else. No wizard had tricked him. No mighty warrior had defeated him. He could blame only himself.

"Hey, Buster!"

Was that another knight who had come to rescue him? No, it wasn't possible. Sir Buster knew that he could not be freed so easily.

"Helloooooo, Buster! Are you there?"

The Brain was calling to him from outside.

Buster looked down.

"Watch this!" said the Brain.

He threw a model airplane into the air. It climbed upward, did a loop-the-loop, and then sailed to a smooth landing.

"Impressive, huh?" said the Brain.

Buster shrugged. "I suppose."

"You *suppose*?" the Brain repeated. "I've been practicing all morning. Most people say throwing is all in the wrist. But it's a lot more complicated than that." He paused. "Why are you inside on such a superlative Sunday afternoon, anyway? Come on out."

Buster shook his head. "I can't," he said. "I have to stay in my room. I'm a knight imprisoned in a castle tower."

"Why?" asked the Brain. "Are you sick?"

"No."

"Too much homework?"

"No."

The Brain frowned. "Do you have other plans?"

"Not exactly."

The Brain scratched his head. "Then what's the problem?"

Buster sighed. "It's a long story."

"Really?" The Brain looked interested. "So what happened?"

"Where should I start?" said Buster. He stopped to think.

"What about at the beginning?" said the Brain helpfully.

Buster brightened. "Yes, that would be a good place. Now pay attention. . . . Once upon a time — well, just the other day — I was sitting in the Sugar Bowl with you and Arthur. . . ."

Chapter 2

· · · · · · · · · · ·

"It's the end of civilization as we know it!" said the Brain. He pretended to cower in the corner of the booth. A mere two feet away, his CyberToy electric robot crashed through a wall of paper cups. "The Cyber-Monster has broken through our last line of defense. His power appears to be unstoppable. What shall we do?"

Across the table, Buster and Arthur were sipping sodas. They looked bored.

"Maybe it'll trip and fall," said Buster.

"Or," said Arthur, "we could wait for its batteries to run down."

"That's right," agreed Buster. "Those CyberToys use a lot of energy."

The Brain was shocked. "What kind of strategy is that? Brave and fearless adventurers do not wait for enemies to trip or batteries to run down. They do something brave and fearless. I'm surprised you guys don't know that." He shook his head. "Maybe you'll feel differently, though, when you get your own CyberToy."

Buster and Arthur looked at each other and sighed.

"That won't be any time soon," said Buster. "My mom says I can't have one until my birthday."

"What about you, Arthur?" the Brain asked.

"They're pretty expensive," Arthur reminded him. "If I want one, my parents say I have to use my own money." He patted his pockets. "And I don't have enough."

Buster sighed again. "Binky has this

great CyberMouse. He put it in Muffy's picnic basket the other day. I can still hear the sound of Muffy's scream when she found it. . . ."

"Some of them are amazingly lifelike," said the Brain. "Many have a full range of moving parts."

"Francine lets her cat play with hers," said Arthur. "Imagine that! A cat has a CyberToy, but we don't."

"Well," said the Brain, "I'm sure some good friend will let you borrow one. . . . Hey, don't look at me. I just got this. Maybe after a while, a year or so, I would —"

"Here you are!" cried Francine, as she and Binky came running into the shop. "Guess what? The toy store just got the CyberToy action sets."

"You mean Creepy Castle?" said the Brain. "With the fully retractable drawbridge?"

Binky nodded. "And the Galactic Garage, complete with space dock and maintenance center. We're going to check them out."

"Any of you want to come?" asked Francine.

The Brain stood up. "Count me in," he said, grabbing his CyberToy. "I hope they're not sold out."

The three of them raced off.

Buster and Arthur didn't move.

"Do you ever get the feeling," said Buster, "that your nose is pressed up against a glass window watching everyone else have a good time, but you're not allowed to join in?" He rubbed his nose quickly. "I think everyone on Earth has a CyberToy except us."

"Come on, Buster," said Arthur. "Not everyone. You're exaggerating."

"I am not."

"Yes, you are," Arthur insisted.

"Oh, yeah? Look!"

Buster pointed out the window. The Tibble twins were walking by with matching twin CyberToys in their arms.

Arthur took a long sip on his soda. "Maybe you're right," he said.

Chapter 3

• • • • • • • • • • • •

"Is there no escape?" said Buster.

He and Arthur were standing in the drugstore at one end of a long aisle.

"You'd think we were safe," Buster went on. "I mean, I've been avoiding the toy store. No point in feeling worse than I have to. But I didn't think coming in here would be dangerous."

"My mother will be done with her errands in a minute," said Arthur. "Meanwhile, close your eyes . . . count to a hundred. Or just turn away. Don't get sucked in."

"Too late," said Buster. Dr. Zontar, the

Mad Scientist CyberToy, was staring at him from the shelf. He had very hypnotic eyes.

Buster picked him up. "This guy is amazing. Look at the craftsmanship. Look at the detail. Look at the power-mad accessories."

"And look at the price," added Arthur.

"True," said Buster.

Arthur noticed some Bionic Bunny puzzles on the next shelf. "What about these?" he said, putting down his backpack. "They're a lot less money."

Buster continued to stare at Dr. Zontar's hypnotic eyes.

The Brain, Binky, Francine, and Muffy were playing with their CyberToys at the Sugar Bowl. Suddenly, there was a heavy knock at the door.

"Stand back!" said Buster. "Make room!"

Everyone looked up. Buster entered and put

Dr. Zontar on the table. Dr. Z spun around and shot out beams of light from his eyes.

"Wow, Buster!" said the Brain. "That's the coolest CyberToy ever."

"I'm not letting it do any experiments on my CyberMouse," said Binky.

"Dr. Zontar is not interested in Cyber-Mice." Buster said quietly. "He's interested in world domination. And he's mine — all mine! HA ha ha ha ha!"

"What are you laughing about?" Arthur asked.

"Oh, nothing," said Buster, feeling the slim hold of world domination slipping away. "So how many pieces does the puzzle have?"

"Let me see," said Arthur.

Buster noticed that Arthur's backpack was open. And Dr. Z was still staring at him. Buster looked back and forth from Dr. Zontar to the open backpack.

CyberToy. Backpack. CyberToy. Backpack.

Then Buster quickly dropped Dr. Zontar into the backpack.

"Oh, here it is," said Arthur. "Only a hundred pieces. Way too easy."

"Yeah," said Buster. "Come on, let's go." He picked up Arthur's backpack, zipped it shut, and handed it to him.

"Hey, I saw that!" said D.W.

Buster froze.

"Saw what?" asked Arthur.

She pointed to the Bionic Bunny lunch box display. "I saw that on TV."

Buster wiped his forehead. "Me, too. I definitely saw it on TV. There's nothing wrong with your eyesight, D.W. Or your memory, either."

"I guess not. Come on, Arthur. Mom's ready to go."

Mrs. Read was waiting with Kate in the checkout line.

"Do you want a ride home, Buster?" she asked.

"No, no, I-I think I'll walk. You want to come with me, Arthur?"

"No, thanks. I've got homework to do."

"Okay." Buster frowned. "D.W., who are you waving at?"

"Up there," she answered, pointing the camera mounted on the wall. "See, Kate? We're on TV. Smile."

"That's not TV," said Arthur. "That's a security camera."

"What's the difference?" said D.W. "Either way, you know someone is watching."

Buster gulped and hurried out of the store.

Chapter 4

As Buster hurried home, he barely noticed anything around him. His heart was pounding, and his eyes were wide-open with dread.

His route took him past the ball field, where Binky and Francine were playing a game with some other kids. As the pitcher wound up to throw, the runner on first base started for second.

The catcher fired the ball over to second as soon as he got it back, but the runner slid in safely.

"He stole second base!" said Binky. "Way to go!"

"Go for broke!" Francine shouted. "Steal third!"

"No stealing!" cried Buster suddenly. "Stealing is bad."

Binky and Francine turned around.

"What are you talking about, Buster?" asked Binky.

Francine frowned. "Are you okay?"

"Oh, sure." Buster shrugged. "Never been better. Just a little caught up in things, I guess. I'll see you guys later."

He ignored their puzzled looks and continued on his way.

"What have I done?" he said to himself. "I'm a criminal."

A siren suddenly wailed as a police car whizzed by.

Buster jumped. They had come to get him. Boy, that was fast! But wait — how could they know he was guilty? They had no evidence. So he was safe. But wait again. There was evidence, after all. It was just somewhere else.

It was night at Arthur's house. But it wasn't dark, because two police cars were parked outside, their lights flashing. A crowd had gathered, and everyone watched as the front door opened.

"He's agreed to come quietly," said one police officer.

"I don't think he wants to cause a scene," said another.

They stepped aside as Arthur made his appearance. His parents, D.W., and Kate looked on in shock.

"I'm innocent, I tell you!" Arthur shouted.

"That's what they all say," said the first police officer.

Arthur looked up at him. "Well, maybe they have a good reason."

"Don't worry, Arthur," said his father. "I

know the food in jail isn't that good. So I'll make you something special."

"Are those handcuffs really necessary?" asked Mrs. Read. "Arthur's always been such a good boy."

"Well, not always," said D.W. "Remember the time —"

"Sorry, ma'am," said the officer. "But when a criminal has itchy fingers, we like to keep him under control. You never know what he might set his sights on next."

"But I didn't do anything," Arthur insisted. "I've been framed! I didn't put the CyberToy in my backpack. I don't know how it got there." He glanced around wildly. "Look! There's Buster! He's my best friend. Buster, tell them I'd never do anything like this. Please!"

All eyes turned toward Buster. He felt like he was under a spotlight.

"Well?" said the police officer. "What about it, Buster? Is Arthur telling the truth?"

Buster cringed under the glare of so many eyes. "I don't know," he said. "Sometimes people do very strange things when they're under pressure."

"Aha!" cried the police officer in triumph. "Take him away!"

Chapter 5

• • • • • • • • • • •

"Good timing!" said Mrs. Baxter, as Buster walked in. "Dinner is just about ready. Go wash up."

Buster was gone for a minute. When he returned, his mother frowned at him. "You know, Buster, you look crooked."

"Crooked?" Buster gulped. "Really? You can tell?"

His mother tilted her head to one side. "Definitely crooked."

"You can see it from there? Across the room?"

"Oh, I think anyone would notice."

Buster gasped. "You do?"

"Certainly. It's the way your shirt is hanging out. If you just ... yes, that's much better."

Buster tucked in the rest of his shirt and hid his reddening face behind a glass of milk.

"Well, I had quite a day," his mother went on. "The trials of putting out a newspaper don't get much attention these days."

"Did you say *trials*?" asked Buster.

His mother nodded. "Two reporters got into a big argument. One accused the other of robbing him of a big story."

"Did you say *robbing*?" Buster asked.

His mother nodded again. "Oh, yes. Voices were raised, I can tell you that. People could probably hear them all over town." She sighed. "Of course, both reporters have been under a lot of pressure. They've done good work lately, and probably feel like they've become prisoners of their own success."

"*Prisoners*," Buster repeated.

*   *   *

"All rise," ordered the court bailiff. "The courtroom of the honorable Judge Ratburn is hereby called to order."

"You may take your seats!" said the judge. "Now, how did you spend your weekend?"

"I studied motion-detecting security systems," said the Brain.

"I read Crime and Punishment," said Francine.

"I went on a field trip," said Binky, "to the police station."

"And what about you, Buster?" asked the judge.

All eyes turned toward him.

"I stole a CyberToy from the drugstore," Buster muttered.

Everyone turned to stare.

"What was that?" said the judge. "Speak up, speak up!"

"I STOLE A CYBERTOY!" Buster shouted.

His friends gasped.

25

"All by yourself?" asked Binky.

"No," Buster admitted. "I used Arthur as an unwitting accomplice."

His friends gasped even louder.

"Well, Buster Baxter," said Judge Ratburn, "you have definitely shown your true colors — or should I say your true stripes."

He banged his gavel sharply — and POOF — Buster looked down to see himself wearing prison clothes.

"Nooooooo!" he wailed.

"Buster, are you all right?" asked Mrs. Baxter.

"Um, sure. Why do you ask?"

"Well," she said, "you have this funny look on your face. And you've arranged your peas into stripes." She took a closer look. "They actually look like the bars of a cage."

Buster looked down. "Or a jail cell," he murmured.

"What was that?"

"Nothing," said Buster. He paused. "I have to go see Arthur."

"Now?" Mrs. Baxter looked surprised. "It will be dark soon."

"I'll be quick. I promise."

"Can't you just call him?" his mother asked.

Buster shook his head. "No, no," he said. "It's complicated. This is the kind of talking that has to be done in person."

Chapter 6

• • • • • • • • • • • •

Buster arrived at Arthur's house a short time later. He glanced around quickly.

"I don't think I was seen," he said to himself. "Now if Arthur will just —"

"Hi, Buster," said D.W., opening the door. "I saw you from the window."

"Don't say hi to me," said Buster. "I'm not here."

"You're not?" D.W. frowned. "It sure looks like you're here."

"Well, looks can be deceiving. Things are not always as they appear."

D.W. looked confused.

"Never mind," Buster said quickly. "Where's Arthur?"

"Right here," said Arthur, coming down the stairs. "What's up, Buster? Gee, you look terrible."

"Maybe he doesn't," said D.W. "Looks can be . . . what was that word, Buster?"

"Deceiving."

She nodded.

"Are you okay?" asked Arthur. "Deceiving or not, you look a little pale."

Buster swallowed nervously. "I need to talk to you. NOW!"

"Okay. What's going on?"

"Not here. We need privacy. Maybe in your cell — I mean, your room."

He darted past Arthur and ran upstairs.

Arthur shrugged at D.W. and followed Buster.

"What's this all about?" Arthur asked, once his bedroom door was closed. "Why are you acting so weird?"

"Um, imagine you had a friend, and this friend did something he shouldn't have.

30

He didn't plan to do it or anything. Some-how it just happened. It was an impulse, a bolt from the blue, a —"

"Buster!"

Buster sighed. "Never mind," he said. "I guess you haven't opened your backpack since you got home."

Arthur shook his head. "Why?"

"I'll show you." Buster picked it up — and pulled out the CyberToy.

Arthur gasped. "Where did that come from?"

"The drugstore."

"And how did it get in my backpack?"

Buster turned red. "I put it there."

"You *what*?"

Buster flopped on the bed, covering his face with his hands.

"I stole it! I know it was wrong, but everyone has a CyberToy except us. I . . . I couldn't help it."

Arthur sat down on his bed. "And you

couldn't help getting me involved, either. That's just great. A stolen toy I didn't even know about is being stashed right here in my room."

"I'm sorry, I'm sorry, I'm *sooooooo* sorry. I didn't want to get anyone in trouble. Not you. Not me. Not anyone. But what do I do now? I don't even want the CyberToy anymore. That's the truth."

Arthur sat down next to him. "Well, what do you usually do when you get something you don't want?"

Buster stopped to think. "Ask for a refund?"

"Yes, well, that makes sense when you've actually *paid* for something. But that's not the case here."

"Oh, right. So what, then?"

"You return it!"

"Ah," said Buster. "Of course. Naturally. That makes perfect sense. We'll return it. That's the only thing to do."

"And it's the right thing to do."

RRRRRRRRRR. The CyberToy suddenly turned on and started walking across the floor.

"Shut that thing off!" Arthur ordered. "And get it out of here!"

"Okay, okay. But then what?"

"You take it back."

Buster blinked. "Alone?"

"You managed to take it that way," Arthur said.

"But, but I had your backpack to help. Couldn't you go with me? Please?"

Arthur took a deep breath. "All right, don't panic. We'll just stop by the store first thing in the morning. If we're lucky, no one else will ever know it was gone."

"And if we're not lucky?" said Buster.

Arthur took a deep breath. "Don't even think about it."

Chapter 7

● ● ● ● ● ● ● ● ● ● ●

The next morning Arthur waited on the street corner for Buster to arrive.

"I don't see why I'm so nervous," he muttered, pacing back and forth. "I didn't do anything. I mean, it was *my* backpack, but I wasn't in on the plan. Not that there was a plan, of course. Buster isn't a criminal mastermind." He paused. "However, a criminal mastermind wouldn't want to throw suspicion on himself. So if Buster was a criminal mastermind, he'd probably pretend to act just like Buster acts now." He looked up. "But that's silly . . . I think."

"What's silly?" asked Buster.

Arthur jumped. "Hey, no sneaking up on me. Friends don't sneak up on each other. Only criminal masterminds do that."

"I wasn't sneaking. I called out your name. You didn't seem to hear me."

"Oh." Arthur looked around. "Where's the *you-know-what*?"

Buster patted his backpack. "Right here, safe and sound." He shuddered. "I had dreams all night of being chased by the thing."

"You do look a little sleepy," Arthur admitted. "Is that why you're late?"

"No, no," said Buster, "I was writing the note. It took me longer than I expected. I went through a lot of drafts."

"What does it say?"

Buster took it out. He cleared his throat.

Dear Drugstore,
We didn't mean to take this CyberToy.

Somehow it just ended up in Arthur's back-pack. It is still like new. You can check.
Unanimous

"*Unanimous?*" said Arthur.

"You know," said Buster. "So no one knows we did it."

Arthur frowned. "I think that's *Anonymous.*"

Buster scratched his head. "Are you sure?"

"Positive. Besides, Buster, you mentioned my name. How *unanimous* or *anonymous* does that make it? It's kind of a big clue, don't you think?"

"Oh, right. I guess I was nervous. Well, we'll fix that."

When they got to the drugstore, Buster put the bag down at the door.

"Okay, let's go," he said.

"We can't just leave it outside," said Arthur. "Someone might steal it."

"As long as it isn't me . . . ," said Buster.

"No, really, Buster." Arthur felt very strongly about this. "It's bad enough that we have to be here at all. But since we are, we have to do this right."

Buster sighed. "Okay, okay. So what's your plan?"

"*My* plan?"

Buster nodded. "If you don't want to just drop it and run, I figure you must have a plan of your own."

"A plan of my own?" Arthur folded his arms. "What you wanted to do isn't a plan. A plan has to have several steps. A plan has to —"

"It was a plan to me," said Buster. "A nice, simple plan. You could call it *Plan A*."

"Well, Plan A isn't going to work," Arthur insisted.

Suddenly the front door opened.

"Good morning," said the pharmacist,

Mr. Gage. "I'm in the middle of taking inventory, but come on in."

Arthur and Buster shared a worried glance, then followed him inside.

"Now on to *Plan B*," Buster whispered.

Chapter 8

• • • • • • • • • • • •

As Mr. Gage went back to checking his stock, Buster pulled Arthur aside.

"So how do we do this?"

Arthur thought for a moment. "I'll keep Mr. Gage busy in the candy aisle while you return the CyberToy. And remember," he added, "the security camera is watching."

Buster nodded and tiptoed away. Arthur made his way over to the candy, where Mr. Gage was checking his supplies.

"I guess candy must come and go pretty quickly here," said Arthur.

Mr. Gage nodded. "It's a sweet spot in

our sales," he said. "Sorry, that's a drug-store joke."

"And a *good* one," said Arthur. "I can't wait to share it with my friends. Does candy change much over the years, though?"

"Well, chewy is still very solid, but sticky is not as popular as it once was. Too many kids with braces."

"Ahhhh," said Arthur. "How interesting."

"EEEEEEK!"

"Did you hear that?" asked Mr. Gage.

"I think it was Buster."

"Well," said Mr. Gage, "we'd better go see what's going on."

They found Buster standing in front of the CyberToy display rack.

It was empty.

"Oh, no!" said Arthur.

Buster just nodded hard.

"Don't worry, boys," said Mr. Gage. "We ran out last night, but I've already got

my new order in." He shook his head. "Everyone wants a CyberToy. But I guess I don't have to tell you that."

Buster smiled weakly.

"If you need anything else, let me know."

He went back to work.

"Now what?" Buster whispered. "If we leave it now, he'll know we brought it!"

Arthur made a face. "Give it to me. Now *you* go look at the candy."

Arthur looked around frantically. Where could he put the CyberToy? Where would a little kid maybe put it and forget about it?

"Aha!" he said.

The Bionic Bunny lunch box display. It was big and blocky. Carefully, Arthur put the CyberToy on the floor behind it. But he was so relieved to be done, he didn't notice the CyberToy starting to walk off behind him.

Arthur returned to the candy aisle.

"All done, Buster?" he asked.

"Uh-huh. Mr. Gage was just explaining the difference between caramel and nougat."

"Come on, then," said Arthur. "We'd better not be late for, um, lunch."

"Hold on there," said Mr. Gage. "Didn't you boys come in for something?"

"Oh," said Buster, "just these law breakers — I mean, Jaw Breakers."

He picked out a few.

"That'll be sixty-five cents," said Mr. Gage.

Buster paid for the candy.

"Thanks, boys."

Arthur and Buster turned to leave. But as they started forward, the CyberToy whirred out from behind an aisle and crossed their path.

"That's funny," said Mr. Gage. "How did this get here?"

Then he saw Buster's note — which was still attached to the back. He began reading.

"I see," said Mr. Gage, tapping his foot. "So whose idea was this?"

"Whose idea?" said Arthur.

"You mean whose idea?" Buster asked.

"I think that's what he meant," said Arthur. "That's why he said it."

"I was just checking," said Buster.

The foot tapping was getting louder. "Boys, I'm still waiting."

"Okay, okay," said Buster. "I did it! Me! Check your security camera. You'll see! I'm guilty, guilty I tell you."

Mr. Gage looked up at the ceiling. "That security camera? It isn't even working." He paused. "But my phone is. And I think I'd better make some calls."

Chapter 9

• • • • • • • • • • • •

Arthur and his parents were standing by the front door of the drugstore. Next to them stood Mrs. Baxter and Buster. All the parents had arrived quickly following the phone calls from Mr. Gage.

While their parents kept perfectly still, Arthur and Buster were shifting their weight from one foot to the other.

"Boys, I know you meant well by returning the toy," said Mr. Gage. "But stealing it in the first place — that was wrong, very wrong."

"If there are damages . . . ," Mr. Read began.

"... we'll pay whatever you think is fair," said Mrs. Baxter.

Mr. Gage held up a hand. "I'm sure you would, and I appreciate that. I also appreciate that this was a momentary lapse of conscience, an act of passion, you might say. I remember, when I was a boy, there was this butterfly yo-yo I wanted in the worst way." He smiled. "I also appreciate that the boys tried to correct their wrong. So I accept their apology. I could, however, use a little help with my inventory the next two Saturdays."

"They'll be here," said Mrs. Read.

"Bright and early," Mrs. Baxter added.

"Excellent," said Mr. Gage. "Then I think we can consider the matter closed."

On the way out, Arthur finally forced out a few words. "I know it was a dumb thing to do. I'm sorry."

"You should have come to us when you found out what Buster did," said his mother.

49

"Even though you didn't take the toy to begin with," his father added, "covering up the theft just made things worse. We're disappointed in you, Arthur. And Buster, too."

"Dumb, dumb, dumb," said Arthur. "It will *never* happen again."

Meanwhile, Mrs. Baxter was walking briskly with Buster in the other direction.

"You're going to have a long time to think about what you did. Arthur was wrong, but he didn't start this, and he was trying to help a friend. You don't have that excuse."

"Well, I wish I did," said Buster.

"Yes, I imagine you do. In any case, I hope you've learned your lesson." She paused. "And what do you think that lesson is?"

"Um, that security cameras are not always on when you think they are?"

"BUSTER!"

Chapter 10

● ● ● ● ● ● ● ● ● ● ● ●

Buster looked down at the Brain.

"And that's why I'm inside on a perfect Sunday afternoon. All because of a toy I just *had* to have."

He shook his head.

"That was some story," said the Brain. "It had action, suspense — and everyone learned a valuable lesson."

"You could say that," said Buster. "My mother says I'm going to be learning my lesson for the next month. Except for school and going to the store on Saturday, I'm stuck at home."

"And so the knight remains imprisoned

in the castle tower," said the Brain. "Still, I have just one question. After making this big mistake and then learning from it, do you think someday you'll get to live happily ever after?"

Buster glanced behind him, where his mother had been listening to him tell the story. She smiled.

Buster smiled back and turned again to the Brain.

"I sure hope so," he said.